JO

FRIENDS
OF ACPL

The Land of Right Up and Down

The Land of Right Up and Down

by

EVA-LIS WUORIO

illustrated by

EDWARD ARDIZZONE

The World Publishing Company

Cleveland and New York

PUBLISHED BY The World Publishing Company
2231 West 110th Street, Cleveland 2, Ohio

PUBLISHED SIMULTANEOUSLY IN CANADA BY
Nelson, Foster & Scott Ltd.

Library of Congress Catalog Card Number: 64-12358

FIRST EDITION

COWP

For my Mother

and her little friends

Pilar, Meritxell, Maribelle, and Xavier

of Arinsal in Andorra

I T WAS a lovely morning. But Maribelle was sad. She sat
on the stone step outside the kitchen door, her chin in
her hands.

Her dog Perro had his head on her knee. But she didn't
pat him.

The cows and the calf mooed in the barn. But she didn't
go to let them out.

The snow-covered mountain peaks, above her, and below
her, sparkled in the morning sun. But she didn't, as she usually
did, wave them a happy greeting.

9

The silver river far down in the valley sang a merry song. But she didn't listen to it.

A cloud of lacy blue butterflies danced around her. But she didn't talk to them.

From the high mountain meadows, far above, her friend Cisco yodeled to her. But Maribelle did not even answer him.

Her mother had been watching her, between her chores. Now she came out.

"Don't be sad, little daughter," she said. "Now and then, in life, everyone of us must meet disappointments. We must meet them cheerfully and bravely."

She stroked Maribelle's thick brown hair and went back to her work.

A blue butterfly landed on Maribelle's hand. It fluttered its wings in the sunlight.

"Little friend," Maribelle said at last, "you can well be gay. You can go to the Fiesta of Our Lady of Meritxell flying there on your pretty wings. We are not going this year at all. We have no way to go. Old Pedro, our good horse, is dead. And it's too far to walk."

Maribelle could feel the tears starting in her eyes. She stood up, but softly, so as not to frighten the butterflies.

"Come along then, little friends," she said. "We'll take the cows up to the high meadows. Come and help me, Perro!"

Vaca, the old cow, came lumbering out of the barn. After her came her calf, and the other two cows. Perro barked at their feet to make them take the right path, behind the house, up the mountain. Maribelle fetched Grandfather's umbrella. In the spring there were often showers. The butterflies flurried in little blue clouds behind the cows.

10

"Your lunch basket, Maribelle!" Mother called.

It was a basket woven of straw, with a blue-and-white checked napkin on top of it. There would be a mid-morning snack and hot soup or stew for lunch as well. Maribelle weighed the basket in her hand and wondered if there was a surprise too. Sometimes there was.

As she started up the path she began to count on her fingers all the things she must remember to do during the day.

Oldest Grandmother wanted some herbs. In the pine woods beyond the fresh meadows, there was just the herb she needed for the pain in her legs. But she herself couldn't walk that far any longer. She had asked Maribelle to gather it for her.

Grandfather liked to have in his stew the cress that grew by the small creeks.

Her mother wanted her to knit at least two inches of baby brother Xavier's sock while she watched over the cows. That would be the hardest thing to do. Maribelle didn't want to look down at an old sock. She wanted to look up, and down, and all around.

Well, that was three things to do. She would remember them all now. It was good to have fingers to count on, whatever the schoolmaster said about people who were nine years old counting with their fingers.

Maribelle climbed on top of the stone fence that edged the path. From up there she was almost as tall as the cows that meandered, one after another, beside her. The path had to be fenced with stones, if it wasn't it might slide right down the mountainside during the early spring rains.

This was because Maribelle lived in a country that went right up and down. Wherever you were going you never

walked just straight on. You were either climbing up, or climbing down.

Maribelle's country is high in the peaks of the Pyrenees mountains. It is called Andorra. The mountains climb the sky. The rivers drop into the valleys of Spain.

The cattle mount up to the high meadows to graze. The children run down to a school built against the side of a mountain, so that three paths lead up to the doors, on three levels.

Clouds come in through the windows of the houses.

Sometimes you can only see up, to the snow peaks and the

sky. Sometimes you can only see down, where the green mountain fields slant, and a narrow road twists to the villages below. It depends where the clouds happen to be floating.

Quite often, people in the valleys below could only see, above them, a roof of clouds, with not a glimpse of the hamlet where Maribelle lived. That's why it was called the Village Above the Clouds.

Maribelle loved her mountains. Of course she had heard at school that there were places without mountains in the world, but she couldn't imagine them.

Now, as she climbed behind the cows, she looked up to the peaks. The mountains seemed to her like good old friends. She began to feel happier.

A boy, far above, yodeled a long call. It echoed against the mountains, "Ma-reee-belllle!"

Maribelle looked up. She smiled. This time she answered, "C-eees-coh!"

The boy's name was actually Francisco, but he was called Cisco for short.

Chapter Two

ALTHOUGH Maribelle had been able to see Cisco, and to hear him call, it took her more than an hour to climb to the meadow where he was.

In the mountains the air is so clear you can see far.

There are no sounds but the wind, and the birds singing, so you can hear even a pan dropping, or the sound of a hammer, from the villages far below.

Cisco was sitting on the stone fence of a meadow pale green with new grass and blue with wild iris.

Behind him grazed his old mare and her colt. The little colt was fawn colored and spindly on its long legs.

"Ola! Olé!" Cisco called. "Bring your herd here! There's plenty of lovely new grass."

He jumped down to open the pole barrier.

"That's a pretty little calf old Vaca has! What do you call her?"

"I haven't named her yet," Maribelle said.

14

"I haven't named the colt either and my father says he's mine. We'll think up names for both of them."

Maribelle nodded. She set the umbrella carefully against the thick trunk of a pine tree. She hung her basket from a branch.

Cisco stood staring at her. Something was wrong, he was sure. Maribelle was usually full of talk.

He didn't ask her. Perhaps she'd tell him.

While the animals grazed, the children climbed up to a little pool in the stream, and picked wild cress for Grandfather's stew. Then Cisco volunteered to climb farther on to the pine woods for herbs for the Oldest Grandmother. Maribelle stayed in the meadow to watch over the herd.

The moment she was alone the butterflies came in clouds to play around her. The bright blue butterflies had stayed below. Here there were purple ones, and yellow ones and orange ones. There were shimmering ones that seemed to be made of thin silver lace. There were spotted ones and striped ones. They danced over the blue iris and the white daisies and the yellow buttercups. They landed on Maribelle's lap and fluttered their delicate wings.

She had to smile.

"Pretty little friends," she said. "Perhaps I'll tell Cisco about my troubles, even though Mother says I must be brave. You are trying to make me happy. He will too."

As it was nearly noon she took her basket from the shady branch. Then she laid the blue-and-white checked napkin on a flat rock. She lifted the lid of the little pot and saw there was enough stew for two. She broke the bread and her small piece of cheese in two.

She heard Cisco's happy yodeling before he came. He didn't call out words. Just high happy sounds like a flute with a tune.

He had taken off his cap and filled it with all sorts of shrubs and plants and leaves.

"Are these all right?" he asked, emptying everything on Maribelle's lap.

"Why, here's the herb the Oldest Grandmother uses for her evening tea," Maribelle said. "She'll be very glad to get that. And these, see, Cisco, are for her rheumatism. These I don't know at all, but I'll take them all down to her. She'll tell us if they are useful."

Cisco opened his leather sack and began to put the food in it on Maribelle's napkin.

"We've sausage sandwiches," he said, "and a tomato. We'll split that. And two apples. And here is some more cheese. We'll have a feast. I'm hungry."

After they had shared everything evenly, Maribelle said, "Cisco, we are not going to the Fiesta of Our Lady of Meritxell this year."

"What do you mean we aren't!" Cisco sat up straight. "Of course we are. We always go. Everyone in all of Andorra goes!"

"I mean us, our family," Maribelle said. "Because Old Pedro is dead and can't take us there."

Canillo, where the Fiesta was held each year, was on a mountain the other side of the big valleys. Most people went by horse and cart because hardly anyone had a car, or money to rent one.

"He was a kind horse," Cisco said, "but never mind. You can go with us. We've always gone together."

"I couldn't go, Cisco," Maribelle said, "not without Grandfather and baby Xavier and Mother and Father. You know that."

"That's true," the boy agreed. Both of them knew that the Fiesta was for all the family.

"Never mind, Maribelle. I won't go either! Or we'll think of something! You'll see!"

He jumped up and began to shoo the cows and the mare higher up the meadow. He could never sit still for long. He was never sad.

Maribelle knew that he would have to go with his family, of course. All the same she suddenly felt a lot more cheerful.

As she began to clear up their lunch an unusual sound came to her ears. It was like the sound of the baker's truck coming up from the village in the valley, only smoother. And today wasn't his day to come to the Village Above the Clouds.

She climbed on the stone hedge.

The hamlet, below, looked as though it had been made from tiny blocks. Yet the air was so clear she could see everything that was happening down there.

By the plumes of smoke from the chimneys she could tell who was cooking lunch. She could see the widow Poblado weeding her vegetable patch. She was very proud of it. The black still figure by the nearest hut would be the Oldest Grandmother taking the noon sun. Her own mother, carrying baby Xavier, had stopped to talk to the women doing

18

the family washing in the pool above the bridge. Uncle Antonio was plowing his tobacco patch with his black oxen.

And far far below, in the valley of the mountains, where the twisty ribbon of a road followed the rushing river, there was a small cloud of dust.

"Cisco!" Maribelle called.

"I see it!" Cisco shouted from above. "It's a car! It's a car that's never been in our village before!"

Chapter Three

ALTHOUGH the mountain tops still flamed in the late sun, it was dusk in the village when the children descended.

All around them rang the soft chorus of cowbells as the herds made their way down from the various pastures. The river roared louder as they came close to it. From the valleys below echoed the Angelus bells of distant churches.

In front of the Poblado, where old Señora Lola kept a couple of rooms for travelers, there stood the strange car. It was pale blue and larger than any private car either Maribelle or Cisco had ever seen.

Old Vaca the cow continued on her familiar way to the barn. Her calf and the other cows followed her. Caballo, Cisco's mare, nudged her colt toward the stables. But the children stood rooted, staring at this unusual sight.

"Blue!" Cisco said. "Think of that! A blue car!"

The few that sometimes came up to their hamlet were invariably black and old.

20

"Maribelle!" her mother was calling from the doorway of the highest house in the hamlet.

"Cisco! Supper!" his mother was calling from the path by the stables.

They had to run.

"See you in the high meadows in the morning!" Cisco shouted as they raced up the cobbled lanes toward home.

But in the morning Maribelle's mother needed her in the village. She herself was going up to the terraced tobacco patches to help Father. Someone had to stay to look after baby Xavier. And also somebody had to be there in case the

21

Tinker Man came. There had been a message from the baker that the tinker had been seen in a near-by hamlet.

"Here are two pots and a pan," Maribelle's mother said. "If he comes, ask him to mend them. And here is a piece of snow-cured ham with which to pay him."

"Do I have time to run down to see the Oldest Grandmother?" Maribelle asked.

"Yes. But run back as quickly as you can."

Maribelle skipped down to the little house two lanes below. Oldest Grandmother was sitting on her stoop in the morning sun.

"I hear you, child," she called while Maribelle was still on the upper lane. Although her legs were weak, her ears were very sharp. "Welcome, welcome!"

"I've brought you some herbs," Maribelle said. "Cisco picked them. There are some strange ones too!"

"Ah, wild thyme," said the Oldest Grandmother, sorting them happily. "Good, very good. And frigola, that's splendid. And marjoram. What's this? Why, he's found some wild radish."

"I'm sorry it's all gone limp," Maribelle said.

"He must have picked it by a rivulet in the meadows. Very useful it is, dried in the hot sun. Ask him to find me some more, there's a good child."

Cisco's mother called to Maribelle as she passed their house.

"Can you come and mind the store for me this morning, Maribelle?" she asked. "Cisco's gone up the high meadows, and I must go and help in the tobacco patches."

Cisco's mother had the only store in the village. She had

it at the far end of her kitchen, and sold such things as matches, and sugar, and salt.

"I think I can come if I may bring Xavier with me," Maribelle said. "I'll ask my mother."

"You do that. And thank you."

Maribelle loved minding the store. There was no trouble about counting out the wrong change. Nobody paid right away. The customers just wrote down in a blue-lined notebook what they took, and paid when they had the money or something to trade. However, Cisco's mother thought it was polite to have someone there to greet them.

"Of course you can help Cisco's mother," Maribelle's mother said, getting her things together to go to the tobacco patches. "But don't let Xavier touch anything. And don't forget to milk the goats in the afternoon. And don't forget to look out for the Tinker Man."

Maribelle counted on her fingers and figured out that there were three things to remember again today. One for her thumb, one for her little finger, and one for the middle finger. It was no fun remembering with the same fingers all the time.

It was going to be a busy day. Maribelle loved busy days.

First of all there was Xavier crawling all over the place keeping her busy. Then she helped Uncle Antonio select just the right sized nails he needed, and mark them in the book. Next came Aunt Pilar to trade a piece of cheese for some sugar. Then one of the shepherds came in to fill his wineskin *porrón*, and buy some tobacco.

Just when Xavier had got into the hearth and was covered with ashes and soot, Señora Lola of the Poblado bustled in.

23

As she helped Maribelle clean up Xavier, she said, "Do you know if Cisco's mother keeps any English tea? Strange how these foreigners are forever asking for tea, a weak watery drink. Now, I prefer a good strong cup of coffee any time."

Searching through the dusty shelves, they found a package that said Koo-Long China Tea.

"That's it, English tea," said Señora Lola triumphantly. "It's for the visitor. She's all the way from America. She asked for tea at five o'clock. Have you ever heard of anything like that!"

Just as she was bustling out—Señora Lola always bustled, busy and important—she remembered something.

"Maribelle! I almost forgot to ask you. Now you are getting to be a big girl and can make yourself useful. I'll let you come and sweep the floors and make the foreign lady's bed while she is here. Of course I'll have to teach you how. Can you learn?"

"Yes, Señora Lola," Maribelle said. She always made her own bed at home.

"Good. Well, speak to your mother and come down in the evening and tell me when you can start. I'll give you enough cloth for a winter coat, for your work."

Cloth was expensive, but Señora Lola's brother kept a dry-goods store down in the great town of Escaldes, in the valley below. It was obviously a good arrangement for everybody.

When there was no one in the store, Maribelle took Xavier out on the wide worn stone step outside. The butterflies came, as always, to play with her. They had been her friends all of her life. She was almost sure she could remember how they had danced about her when she was a baby in her cot.

She was sitting there when she heard a rattling and a banging and a shouting. It got louder and nearer. It could be none other but the Tinker Man coming on his visit.

Sure enough, that's who it was.

Black and bent and scowling under his big black hat, he led his little donkey into the square. You could hardly see the donkey for all the things piled on its back. Only its ears twitched tall among the pans and braziers and baskets.

The Tinker Man banged pans together and shouted. The

donkey whinnied and brayed loudly. Windows flew open in the high, narrow gray stone houses.

Down the steep cobbled lanes ran the women of the hamlet, their kettles and pans, iron tubs and ladles, pots and lids, rattling and clanging. All the men who were in the lower meadows stopped working, scratched their heads, put down their scythes and harrows, tethered up their horses and oxen, and started down the mountainsides. Even the smallest children came tumbling down from their homes.

The Tinker Man·went into all the villages of Andorra with news to tell of everyone's friends and relations. He knew what was going on, and everyone was anxious to hear his tales.

Maribelle got there first, with the two pots and one pan in her right hand, and Xavier and the piece of snow-cured ham under her left arm.

"Humph," said the Tinker Man. "That'll do fine. I'll give you a new ladle in change."

Unexpectedly he smiled at Maribelle and she was never again frightened of his big black hat, nor all the noise he made coming and going.

Cisco's mother too came down to give her things to mend to the Tinker Man.

As soon as her pots and the pan were done, Maribelle climbed up home to the highest house in the hamlet. She was glad to get there. She was just in time to milk the goats.

They were bleating behind the corral, happy to see her, because goats love company. She tied Xavier into the chair Grandfather had made for him. Then she let the goats out. They came to gambol by the kitchen step. Maribelle milked into a big blue enamel jug. Xavier laughed to see it.

26

Then she put kindling into the stove, poured water into the big kettle, and lit the fire. Next she set the long wooden table by the windows that looked over the narrow valley to the morning mountains. And right then she heard the welcome call of her mother.

"Olaa! Coming home! Maribelle! Xavier! We are home!"

Maribelle told all about her day while Mother cooked supper.

"That's a splendid idea, to work for a new winter coat," her mother said. "Of course you must help Señora Lola. We'll manage all right. You'll see."

While they were still eating, Cisco rushed in. He was laughing and shouting. His face was rosy with the sun and he was quite breathless.

"Do you know the funniest thing! It's a *lady* that drives the big blue car. A lady! From foreign lands. And do you know something even stranger! You won't believe me! She is here to catch butterflies!"

"What?" said Father, surprised.

"Butterflies?" said Mother. "You can't even eat them."

"Yes, yes, she collects them!" Cisco bounced with excitement.

"Oh, no," said Maribelle.

"Let's go down and see her, Maribelle! Come on, come on!"

"No," said Maribelle. "I'm not going."

Cisco was so surprised he stopped bouncing.

"Why ever not?" he demanded.

"Butterflies are my friends," Maribelle said. "I don't want her to catch them. I don't even want to see her!"

And she ran upstairs to her own room.

27

When Cisco, puzzled about the way girls acted, had gone, Maribelle's mother went up to find her.

"Mother," Maribelle said, "please, I don't have to go to make the foreign lady's bed, do I? I don't have to go and sweep her floor, do I?"

Maribelle's mother sighed. It would have been very nice for the child to have a really *new* coat. It would have helped a lot. But after all, she had intended cutting up a coat of her own for Maribelle, and she could still do it.

She stroked Maribelle's hair.

"You don't have to go, of course not," she said. "It's all right, small daughter. Don't cry."

Chapter Four

THE NEXT morning Maribelle's mother awakened her earlier than usual.

The mountain peaks were turning pink, but the sun was still behind them. The air was clear and cold. Only in the kitchen was there warmth, for already in the open cooking-hearth the fire was blazing.

"Child," Maribelle's mother said. "I want you to go up to the Borda today. Grandfather has been cutting the hay there for a week and he's bound to be short of bread. I'll make a basket of food for you to take to him."

"And you can take up Vaca and her calf as well," said Maribelle's father. "She's big enough for the journey now. They can stay in the upper pastures for the summer."

"Lovely," said Maribelle. She loved going up to the Borda. "How long will I stay with Grandfather?"

Maribelle's mother and father had been talking the night before, after she had gone to bed. Mother had told Father how disappointed Maribelle had been to learn that they couldn't go to the Fiesta of Our Lady of Meritxell this year. On top of this had come the foreign lady to catch butterflies. And because of the way Maribelle felt about that, she would be losing her new coat, too, even before it was earned. They had agreed that a change would be good for their little daughter.

"I'll come and get you in a week or ten days," Maribelle's father said. "I can bring up more provisions for Grandfather at the same time. Are you sure you'll find the way?"

Even though you could see the Borda—a little hut close to the snow peaks—from the hamlet, the way up was long, and hard.

"Oh, yes, Father," Maribelle said. "And so does Perro."

Perro thumped his tail. A few nights before he'd run up alone, just to say hello to Grandfather. He'd take care of his little mistress and the silly cows, all right.

Maribelle's mother handed her a basket. She had packed new bread and cheese, meat and sausage, a tiny packet of coffee and sugar, some bitter chocolate, and a wineskin into it. She wrapped a thick scarf around Maribelle's neck and fetched the umbrella. You could never tell when a rain cloud would come.

Maribelle's father opened the barn door. Vaca was still looking sleepy. Her calf was fast asleep. But drowsily she nuzzled it out.

"Look after the calf now," Father said. "Don't go too fast. Perro will help you."

Perro was a wise shepherd dog. He was so shaggy you could hardly tell which end of him was which. He was old now, so he didn't have to do too much work. But he knew the safe paths up the mountains better than many people, and he could make the cows and the sheep obey him.

30

He led the way. They took the steepest path behind the house. It rose like an escalator. Step by step they climbed higher. Fields, not flat, but sharply sloping, edged the path. Butterflies danced above the flowers.

Maribelle skirted the fields toward a height of rocks and pine. From there she could follow the bottom of a dried cascade where embedded stones would give the animals a foothold.

When the sun was high above the eastern peaks she sat down to rest. Vaca grazed gratefully and Maribelle had a piece of bitter chocolate.

A little farther on they came to a rivulet tinkling down. Maribelle lay flat on her stomach and drank out of her cupped hands. All the animals had a drink too.

At noon they rested again, in the shade of an ancient pine tree. Maribelle ate the sandwiches her mother had made for her. Perro lay down with his head in his paws. The little calf lay down too.

Old Vaca gazed peacefully about her. She had come up the mountain many a summer. She knew she was going to pleasant pastures. It didn't matter to her that the way was long.

They climbed on again.

Afternoon shadows began to stretch across the valleys below. Maribelle was growing tired.

And then, abruptly, the path twisted over the last cliff face, and they came to a peaceful meadow. In a little hollow there

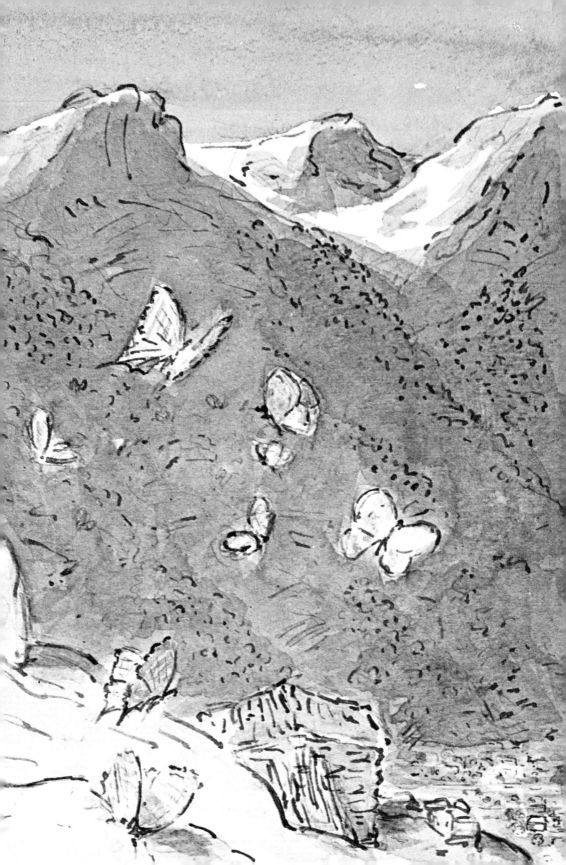

was a hut made of gray stone and weathered thick logs. This was the Borda.

Vaca mooed happily. She knew the place of old. She knew that behind the hut which sheltered Grandfather when he came to cut the hay, and the shepherds when they brought their sheep across the mountains, there was a warm barn for her. Here the grass was wonderfully tasty. She nudged her tired calf-child to the end of the journey.

Perro threw himself flat on the grass and panted. What a good job he'd done again! They'd certainly have been lost without him.

Maribelle sat down on the low stone stoop of the hut. She drew in a long breath. The air in the mountains tasted like a drink of cold water when you were thirsty. Everything around her sparkled with clarity, from the smallest flower to the highest cloud. And far, far below her was her home hamlet.

Up here the mountains leaned down to talk to you.

There was snow only two fields away. The fields were blue with forget-me-nots, like a piece of a fallen summer sky.

It had been a long climb. Maribelle's eyes closed. Butterflies danced in the afternoon sunlight around her.

A familiar shout woke her up.

"Oy-ooh-olay!"

Down the mountain came Grandfather, a scythe over his shoulder, a little red colt running after him. "Just in time for *merienda,* my child," he called. "I've got a pot of stew on, and old Vaca will give us good milk. Won't you, good girl?"

Maribelle ran to the tall old man and wrapped her arms about his waist. Her head didn't reach up to his chest, he was so tall.

Together they went into the hut. Bubbling caldrons and iron pots hung on hooks above the fire laid on the floor. While Grandfather attended to the cooking, Maribelle carried two wooden stools outside.

It was still warm in the sun. The sweet smell of freshly cut hay drifted in the fresh breeze.

When Grandfather brought out the stew she held up their two deep wooden bowls. Then, with his thin long-bladed clasp knife, he cut them both a large slice of bread. Maribelle could hardly wait for the stew to cool, she was so hungry.

"May I sleep in the hayloft tonight?" she asked between spoonfuls.

34

When you put a blanket over the hay you sank into the softest bed. It was a little prickly of course. But you could see stars through the cracks in the rafters, and the mountains whispered to you in the night.

"Yes," Grandfather said. "In the dried hay. If you wish."

"I've missed you, Grandfather."

"I've missed you too, child. But it's good to be here, above the world and all its troubles, here at the Borda."

"It's the best place in the world," Maribelle said.

They smiled contentedly at each other.

Chapter Five

ONE DAY, when Maribelle and Grandfather were having their supper by the hut, they had a surprise.

A happy yodel sounded close and clear.

A few minutes later Cisco climbed up the cliff face, over the last boulders, onto their meadow plateau.

He was carrying a big sack. He was panting a little from the climb, but he was as merry as ever.

"Ola, Grandfather! Olé, Maribelle!" he shouted happily. "I can stay all night!"

"And welcome," said Grandfather.

"Your mother sent some provisions, but she says I must take Maribelle down tomorrow," Cisco said. "She needs you. Wait until you see what I've got!"

Busily he began to empty the sack.

There were things to eat and to store at the hut. There were the nails Grandfather needed to fix the rafters of the hayloft. There was a new bell for Vaca's little calf. And at the bottom of the sack there was a book.

"Look, Maribelle," Cisco shouted. "It's about butterflies."

It was a big flat book and when Cisco opened it, there was a double page of colored pictures.

"Butterflies!" Maribelle gasped. "Why, I know that one! And that one! They are pictures of *my* butterflies!"

"Only some of them are here," Cisco said. "That's why the Butterfly Lady came from America. To find the ones that aren't yet in this book."

"Oh," said Maribelle. She turned away and pretended to be interested in clearing away their mugs and bowls.

"I told the Butterfly Lady," Cisco went on eagerly, "how much you loved butterflies. So she said I could bring the book up for you to see. Wasn't that kind?"

Maribelle didn't say anything. Grandfather pulled at his pipe and looked at the children. Maribelle had told him all about everything.

He said, "That was very kind of the Foreign Lady. May I see the book, Cisco, son."

"Isn't it splendid!" Cisco leaned against the old man's shoulder and pointed with his stubby brown finger. "Look, there! And there!"

"Indeed and truly," Grandfather said. "They are the butterflies of our mountains. Look, Maribelle. Come here, little daughter."

Reluctantly Maribelle leaned over the book. But her eyes brightened at the sight of the pretty pictures.

"That's the one that plays in the high meadows," she said. "And those are the morning ones around home."

"Papilio Machaon," Cisco spelled out. "Those are the blue ones with lacy edges. Parnassius Apollo . . . they are difficult names, aren't they?"

Grandfather suddenly laughed. On his knee there was a small shower of color on wings. His finger pointed at its picture in the book, "Lysandra!"

"The big yellow ones with black stripes and a red spot are Papilio Sinon, look," Cisco said.

"I don't care *what* they are called," Maribelle cried. "I love them all! And *she* wants to catch them."

It had been so happy and peaceful at the Borda. She had forgotten, or at least nearly forgotten, about not being able to go to the Fiesta of Our Lady of Meritxell. She was no longer feeling so sad about the new coat that was to have been and she had quite forgotten about the cruel Foreign Lady who had come to trap her butterflies.

She wished Cisco had not come to see them.

Even Cisco was upset. "Maribelle," he said. "Don't feel like that. It's very interesting, truly it is. I'll tell you how butterflies are born. I bet you never thought of that. And what happens afterward . . ."

But Maribelle had turned away.

Cisco looked at Grandfather, and Grandfather looked at Cisco, man to man.

Then Cisco left at a run. In a minute he was back. He had a limp weed in his hand. It was a piece of wild radish that grew by the rivulet behind the Borda.

"Look, Maribelle, look here now," he commanded.

He stuck it under her nose, and peered down to make sure her eyes were open.

"Do you see those little eggs, sort of, under the leaves? Well, I'll tell you something! They get to be butterflies in the end!"

"You're silly," said Maribelle.

"Come here," said Cisco. "Sit here by me. I'll show you. It's all in the pictures."

Cisco opened the book. After a few minutes Maribelle forgot about everything else.

First there were pictures of the eggs. Tiny little ones, smaller than the head of a pin. Then there were caterpillars, all sorts and sizes. They had grown from the eggs.

"You wait," said Cisco. "I'll show you. The caterpillars are going to grow into butterflies! Oh, yes, believe me! It's almost as though the caterpillars were the grandfathers of the butterflies, the Foreign Lady said."

Grandfather smoked his pipe and smiled to himself.

"Then, look here, Maribelle. Then come the chrysalids. See the pictures? We've seen hundreds of them and wondered what they were. They make sort of a silk net around the caterpillar and hang off branches. You remember how we've found them, with raindrops shining on them?"

Maribelle nodded. She was too interested to speak.

"Now watch, on the next page!" Cisco made sure she was looking. "See! The butterfly breaks the net and comes out flying."

"Dancing," said Maribelle.

"All right, dancing," Cisco said, glad that at last she was sharing this wonderful new game with him. "That's how it all happens."

"*Fabuloso,*" said Grandfather, puffing his pipe.

"I've lots more to tell you," Cisco said. "But I must tell the strangest story first. You know the large blue butterflies you love the best?"

"I love the *little* blue ones best," Maribelle said.

"Well, all right, the blue ones." Cisco wanted her to listen. "And you know that thyme-herb we picked for the Oldest Grandmother?"

"Yes. She wants more too."

"Anyhow, Maribelle, wherever the thyme grows, the blue butterflies lay their eggs."

"Like chickens?" Maribelle asked.

Cisco looked at Grandfather. He nodded.

"Something like chickens," he said.

"And then, remember the day," Cisco continued, "that I went into the pine woods to pick the herb and got bitten by ants? Remember, I stepped on a lot of them, I was so angry. Well, I'm not going to step on any more ants. Do you know why?"

Maribelle just stared at him. Cisco was always stepping on ants and beetles and bugs. She'd often been angry with him about it.

"I'm not going to step on them," said Cisco slowly and loudly, "because they pick up the butterflies' eggs and carry them to their nests and keep them warm and safe all through the long winter. And in the spring the eggs come out and get to be caterpillars and grow into chrysalids, and then, one warm day—BOING—they fly out as butterflies!"

All evening the children sat and looked at the book and talked about the pictures.

Vaca brought her calf to see them, but they barely said hello to the friendly cow. So she stood nearby, munching companionably at her cud, and keeping an eye on her child. Perro lay down at their feet and listened to everything. He was a wise old dog, but he was always willing to learn more. The little colt galloped around a bit and then went to bed.

Finally, when Grandfather had seen that the animals were safe in the barn, he brought the children a piece of bread and chocolate and a mug of milk each.

"The sun's gone behind the mountains," he said. "Look, it's already dusk in the valley of home. Time to sleep for all."

Cisco closed the book.

"Maribelle," he said, seriously. "When we go down to the hamlet tomorrow, you *will* come to see the Butterfly Lady, won't you? Now?"

Maribelle thought about it. She still didn't know whether she wanted to or not.

Grandfather, sitting on his own stool behind them, puffed at his pipe. Then he said, "This Foreign Lady has come here not to destroy your friends the butterflies. She has come to learn more about them. Sometimes life is difficult to understand. But you can see now, can't you, how much pleasure the sight of the pictures has given you, and can give to a lot of other children, far away. No one can paint a butterfly in flight. Not all the people in the world can come up to our mountains to see them. A butterfly's life is a short one, and if you really think about it, I'm sure you'll believe that they'd like to be remembered in such wonderful pictures."

"*Must* she catch them and kill them, to draw them?" Maribelle asked.

42

"I'm afraid, perhaps, she must," Grandfather said. "The ways of knowledge are strange and beyond my understanding. But I think she is doing a good thing, not a bad one."

Maribelle carried the dishes into the hut. When she had finished washing up, the first stars were already out above the familiar peaks.

She looked at them and sighed. It was difficult to begin to understand all these grown-up things.

But she would try. And she would be brave about the Fiesta of Our Lady of Meritxell. And she would try to understand what the Butterfly Lady was doing.

"Good night, dear Grandfather," she said, "Cisco, I'll come with you to see the Butterfly Lady when we go down to the valley tomorrow. Good night."

Chapter Six

ALWAYS, afterward, Maribelle would think of that summer as the Butterfly Summer.

When she and Cisco came down the mountain, the Butterfly Lady was standing on the little balcony of the Poblado. It hangs over the river, so that the song of the rapids almost shivers through you. Maribelle had often stood there, listening with all her heart.

Now the Foreign Lady, who curiously enough, spoke Spanish, called to them.

"Come along here, Cisco, Maribelle! The rapids have a new song tonight."

The Foreign Lady was small and thin. She had kind gray eyes and her smile had a welcome.

They listened to the river singing.

"It's singing of trout," Cisco cried. "I'll get my pole and catch some."

He ran off to fetch it.

44

"It's singing of the snows of the far peaks," Maribelle said. "That's why the river's so high."

"Every evening since I've been here," the Butterfly Lady said, "I've listened. And do you know, every night the river sings a new song."

"That's true," Maribelle agreed. "I've listened to it since I was little. And every time I listen, I hear a new story."

From that moment they were friends.

Maribelle even got used to the fact that her small butterfly friends had to be caught with a net, and that they had to be put into killing bottles so they would keep their color and shape forever.

Cisco made himself one from an old jam jar. He gathered laurel leaves and chopped them up. These he put into the bottle. Then he cut out a round piece of cardboard and stuck it into the bottle over the leaves. If you popped the butterfly there, it would painlessly go to sleep forever.

"They often sit on laurel bushes by themselves," he said defensively when Maribelle said it was cruel. "They just go to sleep happily, that's all."

Afterward, Cisco made a collecting box out of an old can. He put a piece of cork in the bottom of it, and on the inside of the lid. When he took the butterflies out of the jam jar, he stuck them onto the cork with a pin.

Then the Butterfly Lady would sit and slowly and carefully paint them. One day they would be pictures in a wonderful book.

They had a lot of fun too.

The first time Maribelle pointed at a butterfly and said, "That's a Zerynthea Polyxena Creusa," old Señora Lola of the Poblado, who heard her, got awfully excited.

"Maribelle, child," she said. "You come right inside into a cool room. Perhaps you'd better lie down. I'll put a cold compress on your forehead. Oh, dear, oh, dear, and your mother away in the pastures today!"

Maribelle and Cisco laughed and laughed.

"It's all right, dear Señora Lola," Maribelle finally got out. "It's just the name of that butterfly that flew by."

46

"I think you'd better go and sweep the floor of the Foreign Lady," Señora Lola said stuffily, although Maribelle had just done it. "Nonsense, all nonsense," she muttered as she bustled away.

But half a minute later she was back with two cups of lemonade for the children. Usually, she never gave anything away for nothing. "Drink that," she said huffily, "and don't stay too long in the sun."

The children talked about a lot of things with the Butterfly Lady. Not only did they learn about their own butterflies, but also many fascinating things about America. And in turn they told her about the winters when the whole hamlet lay deep in snow, and no one could come up from the valleys below, for weeks, not even the bread truck. Then, they told her they'd remember her and the sunshine days in the high meadows.

And, when the time got close to the day of the Fiesta of Our Lady of Meritxell, Cisco told her about that too, and about Old Pedro the horse that had died, so Maribelle and her family wouldn't be going this year.

"But I don't mind so much any more," said Maribelle. "Mother was right. If you try to be brave about a disappointment, well, it isn't so big after all, is it?"

And then the accident happened.

Maribelle had been minding Xavier and the goats all day. Cisco had been up in the tobacco patches helping his mother. The Butterfly Lady had started out, up the steep mountain, beyond the rapids, all alone. She had stumbled. Her foot had caught between slippery boulders. She hadn't been able to get up.

It was lucky Grandfather was coming down, by a long route, from the Borda that day. He heard her calling. He carried her down to the hamlet.

Everyone came that evening to see how she was. The Butterfly Lady had lived with them the whole summer, and they had all grown to like her. In the mountains people look at you a long time, and think about you, before they decide to be friends.

Everyone was sorry for her.

When for a moment she was alone with Maribelle and Cisco, she said, "Oh, dear, oh, dear."

"Does it hurt terribly?" asked Maribelle.

"It isn't that," said the Butterfly Lady. "It's that now I'll *never* be able to paint the Erebia. That's the butterfly I went looking for again today."

"You haven't told us about the Erebia at all," Cisco said.

"No, because you can only find it in the heights, nearly at the snow line," the Butterfly Lady said.

"Is it pretty, like the Amandus, all shimmering?" Maribelle asked.

"Or black and red and yellow, like Thais?" Cisco shouted. "Or like Colias who flies to visit us all the way from Africa, all bright yellow with brown wing tips?"

The Butterfly Lady had to laugh.

"You are clever children," she said. "You are a joy, both of you. But no, Erebia is nothing like that. It is just a tiny little brown butterfly, with the smallest little black spot on each wing. It's very, very rare. I was so hoping finally to find one."

And right then the doctor came in his car to take her into the big town in the valleys, to look after her foot.

Chapter Seven

MARIBELLE woke up very early. The sky was pale green with dawn. She sat up in bed.

She knew she had dreamed of something important.

She suddenly remembered what it was.

She had seen, up near the Borda, a tiny brown butterfly with a black spot on its wing. It could only have been the Erebia!

She bounced out of bed in her excitement.

How glad the Butterfly Lady would be, to get an Erebia! But—and Maribelle stopped bouncing—who would catch it? She didn't want to. While she did try to understand that for the sake of learning about butterflies they had to be caught and studied, she just didn't want to catch one herself.

Cisco could do it! She would tell him where to find the Erebia!

Then she remembered that Cisco had to go with the herd to the upper meadows this morning.

What was she going to do!

Right then she heard a soft gay whistle. Grandfather was home! He was always up before anyone else. He said that he liked to see the morning star fade and to greet the day before people made it loud.

Maribelle didn't even stop to get dressed. She ran downstairs. Grandfather had climbed on the cliff behind the house to watch the dawn. Maribelle explained everything to him. He puffed at his pipe and thought for a while.

Then he said, "Well, my child, I think the only thing to do is for you to come up to the Borda with me today."

The way up was quicker and shorter with Grandfather. With the animals, you had to wait for them, and be careful not to miss the right paths. But Grandfather went surely. They were at the Borda by noon.

Clouds of butterflies came to meet them. It was now the time for their last sunlit days.

Maribelle could hardly bear to greet them. They had always been her friends. As she sat down to rest, they came as always, in a friendly dancing cloud to play with her.

"Little friends," Maribelle said. "What shall I do?"

A big handsome butterfly landed on her hand.

"I'm sure you know all about my problem," Maribelle told it. "So if I'm really going to catch a little Erebia, I had better get it over and done with, and do it right now."

She started out resolutely, away from the pretty large butterflies, but they all came with her. Shimmering wings led her up a path she had never taken before. She followed where the butterflies led her.

She crossed the meadow of the forget-me-nots, and the little rivulets that ran down from the snowcaps. She went on, and on, to where the bare rocks began, brown and sunbleached. The snow-tipped mountain peaks were very close now.

Maribelle was getting tired. When she found a flat rock she sat down to rest. Perro suddenly came panting up, and threw himself down at her feet. He was a dog who always looked after his people. The butterflies fluttered around her.

Then, brown against a brown rock, she saw the Erebia.

It sat quite still, a tiny brown butterfly with a black spot on each wing tip.

Maribelle sat just as still. Never in her life had she even wanted to catch a butterfly. Now she felt that she just couldn't do it.

The tiny brown Erebia did not move at all.

I haven't got a net, Maribelle thought. I haven't got a killing bottle. I haven't got a collecting box. Of course I can't catch it.

But even as she was thinking this, Maribelle put out her hand, softly, softly. Gently, gently. And picked up the little brown butterfly.

It was very perfect, and very still.

Maribelle knew she wouldn't have to hurt it. The first frost had touched it in the night. She felt proud and content.

As they went down to the Borda, a big blue butterfly swung from Perro's ear, and all the others followed. They were all, still, Maribelle's friends.

A Surprise

IT WAS the seventh of September. Maribelle had never known such a sad seventh of September.

All through the Village Above the Clouds, there were wonderful cooking smells. Everyone was preparing for the picnic of the Fiesta of Our Lady of Meritxell the next day.

All through the mountainous land of Andorra, in the hamlets in the heights and in the towns in the valleys by the roaring rapids, people were making ready for the one great Fiesta of the year. Those who had no new dresses had washed their best old ones. Those who had no new suits had asked their mothers to press their Sunday ones. Everyone was shining up the harness of the horses, and the carts and the carriages and the cars.

In the morning they would start early and make their way to Canillo, where, lost for the rest of the year on the side of a faraway mountain slope, there was the little sanctuary of Our Lady of Meritxell. Only on the day of the fiesta did the mountainside come alive. People flowered upon the brown rocks, picnicking and singing.

54

Maribelle's little brother Xavier crawled to the door step and snuggled against her. So Maribelle picked him up—though he was a fat baby and getting heavy—and said, "At least I can *tell* you the story of Our Lady."

She hugged him and added, "Never mind, Xavier, next year we'll be able to go, for sure."

Cisco ran up, finely dressed, to show her his new suit.

Maribelle said, "I'm telling Xavier the story of the Day of Our Lady."

"I'll listen too," Cisco said. He took a handkerchief out of his pocket, spread it on the step, and sat on it. His mother had told him not to sit on *anything* in his new suit.

"It was like this, Xavier," Maribelle said, rocking her small brother, "long long ago a shepherd boy was minding his sheep

55

on the high slopes at Canillo. He stopped to have his bread at lunch time by a flowering wild rose bush. And do you know what! He found, right there, a statue of Our Lady. It was carved of dark wood, and She was very beautiful.

"Well, he was from Encamp, *down* the mountain a bit. So he took Her home. Everyone loved Her. But next morning when they woke up, She had disappeared!

"And do you know what, Xavier! She was right back under the flowering wild rose bush when he took his flock there.

"That night he had to take some of the goats and sheep *up* the mountain to the houses at Canillo. So he took Our Lady there too.

"But, can you believe it, that night She disappeared again.

"When he went to look for Her, there She was, back on the bare hillside close to Her flowering roses.

"So the people from all over Andorra realized that Our Lady wanted to stay by the high slopes on the mountainside near Canillo and they built a little house there for Her. That's the Sanctuary where we won't be going this year, Xavier."

Cisco jumped up.

"I hear the baker's bus!" he shouted. "I'm sure that he'll have some cakes for us to take on the picnic!"

He was so excited he forgot all about Maribelle. He ran down the path as fast as he could.

Maribelle's mother came out of the house. "Here, child," she said. "Here are five pesetas. Go and see if the baker will sell us some sweet biscuits for tomorrow."

All the village was down at the small square by the bridge. Everybody had ordered cakes and cookies, fruits and preserves for tomorrow. Maribelle hoped no one would ask her if her family was coming too.

56

The truck creaked and puffed to a stop. The baker jumped out.

Everyone began to clamor for his order. But the baker lifted up his hand. When there was silence he called, "Where's Maribelle? Is young Maribelle here?"

"She's here, she's here," shouted Cisco.

"Good," called the baker. "Have you any helpers, Maribelle? There are a lot of packages for you!"

"I'm here!" Cisco shouted. "I'll help!"

"Here and here and here and here!" shouted the baker, handing out large parcels from the back of his truck. "And here is another one! And here's still another one!"

"For me?" said Maribelle. "Are you sure they are for me?"

"That's what it says on the parcels," the baker shouted.

"Read for yourself! Maribelle Montané, House of the Mountains, Village Above the Clouds! That's how I read it. And I've got a message for your mother as well. I'll be coming up when I'm finished here. Ask her to put a pot of coffee on, do."

Grandfather came out of the crowd. He had been meaning to buy something from the baker to surprise the children. Now he shouldered the biggest parcels. Cisco took two others. Maribelle carried two more.

They climbed the path between the houses to their own home. At the door was Mother, with Xavier in her arms.

"What was all the shouting down there," she wanted to know.

"Look! Look!" Maribelle called.

Cisco bounced with excitement. "There is a letter fastened on this box! It's for you, Maribelle!"

They all stood expectantly while Maribelle opened it. She read aloud.

"Dear Maribelle, here are some things for you and your family, for the Fiesta of Our Lady of Meritxell. There is a little box for Cisco too. I do wish I could have come with you all, but the time has come for me to fly back to America. With love from your friend,

The Butterfly Lady"

Oh, the Butterfly Lady should have been there. It was such a lovely morning. Everybody gathered around Maribelle. Then they opened the parcels on the wide stone step, outside the door of their home which was the highest house in the village. The mountain peaks smiled down at them.

58

There were boxes of fruits and preserves. There were cakes and chocolates and candies. There was rice and coffee, sugar and tea. Then there was the box for Cisco, with a splendid folding fishing rod and some flies for trout fishing. There was also a packet of pipe tobacco for Grandfather.

In the biggest box there was a pale blue dress for Maribelle and a new suit for Xavier.

Who would have believed it all!

As they were still looking at everything the baker climbed up to the house. "Ola! Olé!" he called. "I've a message for you from the town below. There has been a car ordered for you to take you to the Fiesta tomorrow. Don't you start walking, now. It's coming bright and early!"

And that's how it happened that Maribelle and all her family went to the Fiesta of Our Lady of Meritxell, like everyone else in all of Andorra.

It was a wonderful Fiesta.

This Is a P. S.

When spring came back to Andorra, and all the millions of butterflies woke up to play with Maribelle, the baker, in his truck, brought her a large flat parcel.

In it was a book with a picture of a little brown butterfly. It looked so alive you'd think it could fly off the page, any minute.

It was Maribelle's Erebia, of course!

ABOUT THE AUTHOR AND ARTIST

EVA-LIS WUORIO lived for ten months of 1956 in Arinsal, a small village of Andorra in the peaks of the Pyrenees, in a house so old and drafty that the villagers called it The House of the Winds. Since then she has frequently returned to the little principality, locally known as The Land Above the Clouds. "The real Andorra," she says, "is in the mountain fastnesses and the tiny villages under the snowcaps, not in the tourist shopping towns. Take any side road up the mountains from the one main highway and you'll find a strange, incredibly beautiful land not of this age or time."

Miss Wuorio was born in Viipuri, an ancient walled Finnish city, and as a child lived in Toronto, Canada. She has been a newspaper columnist, magazine editor, foreign correspondent, and has written fiction for adults and children. Her first children's book published in the United States was *The Island of Fish in the Trees*. Miss Wuorio now lives in London and Ibiza, in the Balearic Islands.

EDWARD ARDIZZONE, an internationally known writer and illustrator of children's books, was born in Vietnam, but has lived in England since the age of five. *Little Tim and the Brave Sea Captain*, written and illustrated by Mr. Ardizzone in 1935, was the first of his many books for children. His book *Tim All Alone*, published in England in 1956, was the first winner of England's Kate Greenaway Medal. In addition, he has illustrated over one hundred books for other authors both here and abroad, including *The Island of Fish in the Trees*. Mr. Ardizzone lives in London.

1 2 3 4 5 68 67 66 65 64